Why Worry?

BY ERIC KIMMEL

ILLUSTRATED BY ELIZABETH CANNON

PANTHEON BOOKS

The song, "A Little Smile"
was written especially
for WHY WORRY?

"A Little Smile" Copyright © 1975 as an unpublished work
(Words) by Shirley Keller, Eric Kimmel and Diane Wolkstein
(Music) by Shirley Keller and Diane Wolkstein
Used by permission.

Text Copyright © 1979 by Eric Kimmel
Illustrations Copyright © 1979 by Beth Cannon
All rights reserved under International and Pan-American Copyright
Conventions. Published in the United States by Pantheon Books,
a division of Random House, Inc., New York, and
simultaneously in Canada by Random House of Canada Limited, Toronto.
Library of Congress Cataloging in Publication Data
Kimmel, Eric A. Why worry?
Summary: When they are snatched up by a crow, a pessimistic cricket and an
optimistic grasshopper disagree about what will happen to them.
[1. Animals—Fiction] I. Cannon, Beth. II. Title.
PZ7.K5648Wh [E] 78-12951
ISBN 0-394-84010-0 ISBN 0-394-94010-5 lib. bdg.
Manufactured in the United States of America
0 8 6 4 2 1 3 5 7 9

For Diane
and Rachel Cloudstone
E.K.

For Frances
E.C.

nce upon a time

there were two good friends, Cricket and Grasshopper, who lived right next door to each other. Grasshopper had an apartment in the trunk of an old hollow tree. Cricket lived in a cozy cellar room beneath a big rock. They were very good friends, but quite different, as you shall see.

Cricket always worried. Grasshopper never did.

One morning Grasshopper called out to her friend, "Good morning, Cricket! Isn't this a fine spring day!"

Cricket poked his head out through the cellar door and sighed. "Oh, I don't know, Grasshopper. I have a feeling something terrible is going to happen today. Something awful!"

"Don't be silly," Grasshopper replied. "What terrible thing could happen on a fine day like this? Come have a cup of tea with me. The kettle is boiling. A cup of tea will do you good."

"Yes," said Cricket weakly. "It might help to calm my nerves."

So he shut the cellar door behind him and set off toward Grasshopper's house.

But no sooner had he stepped onto the path leading to the hollow tree, when a great ugly crow flew down and snatched him up.

"I knew this would happen,"
Cricket said as the crow flew away
with him.

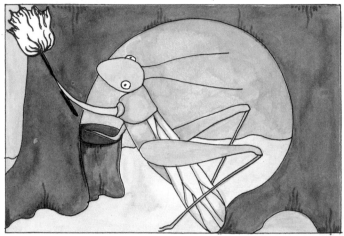

"Let him go, you stupid horrible bird!" Grasshopper cried, shaking
her feather duster at the crow.

The crow swooped down and snatched her up too—feather duster
and all!

"Oh, I'm sorry to have gotten you into this mess," Cricket said sadly.

"Please don't apologize," Grasshopper told him. "What are friends for? Anyway, everything is bound to turn out all right. You'll see."

No sooner had she spoken when the crow sneezed!

Grasshopper's feather duster had been tickling his nose, so that try as he might he couldn't help throwing back his head and letting out a thunderous AAAAAAAAAAAAHHHHHHHCHHHHHHHOOOOOOO!!

Cricket and Grasshopper flew from his beak and tumbled head over heels through the air.

"Oh, oh! We'll be smashed to bits!" Cricket cried. "I can't bear to look."

"Just close your eyes, dear," Grasshopper said. "Don't worry. We'll come out swimmingly."

And they did.
With a great splash the two friends fell right into the middle of a pond.

"There!" said Grasshopper to Cricket. "Didn't I tell you not to worry?"
"But I can't swim!" bubbled Cricket, struggling in the water.

"Why, neither can I," said Grasshopper calmly, as she slowly sank.
"But I am certain something will turn up."

And do you know?
Something did.

A fish came along and swallowed them both
—in one gulp.

"It's awfully dark in here," Cricket whispered after a while.
"Yes. It certainly is," Grasshopper agreed. "Rather musty too."
Cricket began to cry. "I feel so nervous and upset," he said.
"There, there," Grasshopper said, putting her arm around him. "Have a good cry, Cricket. You'll feel better afterward."

"Oh, I knew this would happen," Cricket moaned. "We'll never get out. We'll be trapped in this horrible place forever."

"Oh, I'm sure we'll get out somehow," Grasshopper said. "We just have to wait a bit, that's all. Let's cheer ourselves up with a song. Do you know the words to *A Little Smile?*"

"Sort of," said Cricket weakly.

"Then let's sing it together," said Grasshopper.

So they began to sing.

Suddenly there was a tremendous tossing and shaking.

"What's going on?" cried Cricket.
"Don't worry," said Grasshopper. "We'll find out soon enough."

Indeed they did.
The fish, biting down on what he thought was a fat succulent worm, was caught on the end of a hook.

He struggled and fought bravely, but it was no use. He was lifted high out of the water and soon lay very very still.

Inside, Cricket and Grasshopper huddled together.

All at once there was a flash of light and the sound of voices.

"Look! There are two bugs inside this fish!"
"And they're still alive!"
"Hurry! Get the jar!"
"Don't let them get away!"

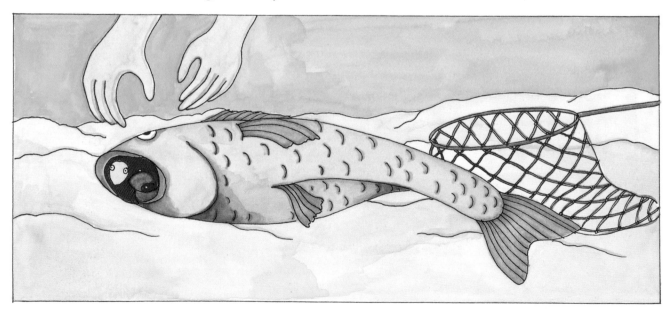

Cricket and Grasshopper were grabbed by a sticky hand and thrust
into an empty jar.

A lid with holes punched in it was quickly screwed on over them. The jar had not been washed very well and bits of chunky peanut butter still clung to its sides.

"Well, this is not too bad after all," said Grasshopper, helping herself to some peanut butter. "Would you care for some too, Cricket?" she asked.

"No, no thank you," Cricket replied. "I don't feel very well. Really. I have a nervous stomach, I'm afraid."

"I've noticed," said Grasshopper sympathetically.

"You don't suppose they'd open the top a bit? Just to let a little more air in?" Cricket asked.

"It never hurts to ask," Grasshopper said, leaping up and down in the hope of attracting attention. "Hello! Hello out there!" she called. "Could you open the lid a bit?"

Slowly the lid of the jar began to turn.
"There!" said Grasshopper, feeling quite pleased with herself.

"Thank goodness!" said Cricket. "I was beginning to feel sick."
"You did look ill," Grasshopper agreed. "Now take a deep breath. It will help."
"Oh! Ask them not to shake the jar," moaned poor Cricket.

Before either one of them could say another word, the two friends were tipped into a plastic bag which was fastened to the bright red tail of a Super Sky Falcon Kite.

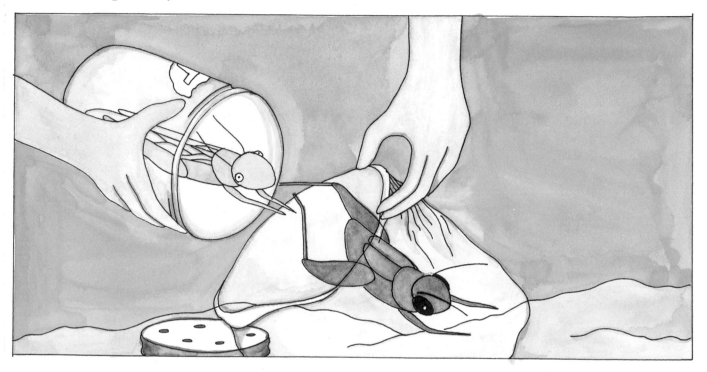

Cricket huddled in the corner of the plastic bag, his eyes shut tight.

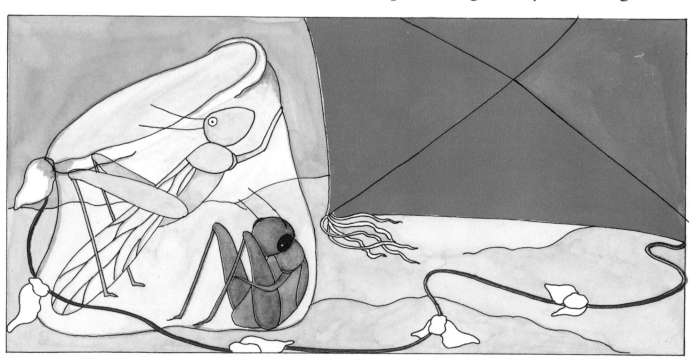

"I feel horrible," Cricket said. "I knew something like this would happen, but like a fool I didn't pay any attention. I just went about my business as if it was an ordinary day. And now what is going to become of us? I should have stayed home. I should never have left my cozy little house."

"Now, now," Grasshopper said. "Why don't we look on the bright side of things. We certainly are seeing quite a bit of the world, aren't we? And when we get home we'll have so many adventures to talk about."

"We'll never get home. Never! Never!" said Cricket as the kite rose gracefully into the air.

"Cricket, come and look! See how high we are! I can see the tops of trees. And look at the pond! It looks like a little drop of dew on the end of a leaf. Oh, Cricket, do open your eyes. I've never seen anything so marvelous in all my life!"

"I think I'm going to throw up,"
said Cricket.

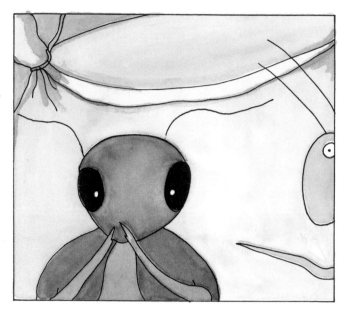

Just then there was a great gust
of wind. The kite string snapped and
the kite sailed higher and higher
into the sky.

Cricket shrieked with fright.

But Grasshopper was not worried at all. "You know," she said to
Cricket, "I've always wanted to fly. And none of this would have hap-
pened if it hadn't been for you. I'm glad we didn't stay home today,
because flying is every bit as lovely as I thought it would be. Don't you
think so?"

Cricket did not answer. He was huddled in his corner muttering, "Heaven help me. Heaven help me," over and over again.

Hours later he opened his eyes. The gliding motion of the kite had ceased.

Cricket looked around.

No, he wasn't in heaven. He was at the top of an old hollow tree into whose branches the kite had nestled. There was something very familiar about the tree, and the stone beside it, far below on the ground.

"Grasshopper! Grasshopper!" Cricket cried, leaping for joy. "Do you know where we are? We're home! We're HOME!"

"Yes," Grasshopper sighed. "I know."

"You don't sound very happy about it," Cricket said.

"Well, it *is* nice to be home again," she replied. "But I was having such a wonderful time, I was hoping it would last a little longer."

"I never thought I'd see home again," Cricket said in a solemn voice, wiping a tear from his eye.

"See," Grasshopper said, taking his hand. "It doesn't pay to worry. Didn't I tell you? Now, why don't we climb down and have that cup of tea."

"I'd be delighted," Cricket said. "But. . . ."

"But what?"

"You don't think it's still too hot, do you?"

"Oh, Cricket!" Grasshopper laughed. "You don't have to worry."

And
do you know?
It was
just right!

ERIC KIMMEL has worked with children as teacher, librarian, and story-teller. His first book, *The Tartar's Sword*, was awarded the Friends of American Writers award. He is also the author of *Mishka, Pishka and Fishka* and contributes to several magazines, including *The Horn Book* and *Cricket*. Born in 1946 in Brooklyn, he has traveled all over the world, and now lives in Oregon where he teaches children's literature and storytelling at Portland State University.

ELIZABETH CANNON studied illustration at the Rhode Island School of Design and has worked as a freelance illustrator and artist since then. She has created the pictures for many books, including *A Cat Had A Fish About A Dream*, a picture-story adventure without words, and *The Seed* by Ann Cameron. Born in 1951, she grew up in Connecticut and is presently dividing her time between Paris and New York.